Buttons

The Dog Who Was More Than A Friend

Buttons

The Dog Who Was More Than A Friend

Linda Yeatman

Illustrated by Hugh Casson

CHILDRENS PRESS CHOICE
A Barron's title selected for educational distribution
ISBN 0-516-08503-4

A percentage of profits will be donated to
The National Hearing Dog Program.

First edition for the United States and the Philippines
published 1988 by Barron's Educational Series, Inc.

First published 1985 by Piccadilly Press Ltd.,
London, England

All inquiries should be addressed to:
Barron's Educational Series, Inc.
250 Wireless Boulevard
Hauppauge, New York 11788

Library of Congress Catalog Card No. 87-35086
International Standard Book No. 0-8120-3956-4

Library of Congress Cataloging-in-Publication Data
Yeatman, Linda.
Buttons : the dog who was more than a friend / Linda Yeatman ; illustrated by Hugh Casson.
Summary: After becoming separated from his human family, a mother and little boy who are both deaf, a puppy is trained as a hearing ear dog and is eventually reunited with his owners.
ISBN 0-8120-3956-4
[1. Hearing ear dogs—Fiction. 2. Deaf—Fiction. 3. Physically handicapped—Fiction.] I. Casson, Hugh Maxwell, Sir, 1910– ill.
II. Title.
PZ7.Y35Bu 1988
[E]—dc19
87-35086
CIP
AC

PRINTED IN THE UNITED STATES OF AMERICA
890 9770 987654321

Contents

Foreword vii
1. A Christmas Present 1
2. Give a Dog a Name 9
3. The Boy Who Didn't Talk 12
4. A Porcupine 15
5. A Sad Picnic 19
6. Lost Dog 23
7. New Friends 28
8. Training 33
9. Alarms and Bells 36
10. Happy Christmas 41
11. A Famous Dog 46

Foreword

Can you imagine living in a silent world — a world in which you would need other people or a hearing aid to alert you to common sounds, such as a doorbell, a ringing telephone, or even a smoke detector?

Nearly two million Americans are severely deaf; an additional 15 million have a substantial hearing loss. For these children and adults, life can be difficult, since deafness is unseen and often misunderstood.

In 1978 the American Humane Association recognized that dogs could be trained to assist the deaf by alerting them to those sounds which many of us take for granted. In addition to actually training dogs, American Humane has helped to establish hearing dog training programs across the country. Today, the Association's National Center for Hearing Dog Information assists local programs through its many publications and training aids. The National Center also helps deaf people find their local training center. Of great importance to the Center is the passage of laws allowing hearing dogs into public places and transportation. Such laws have now been passed by a majority of states.

For many deaf people, a hearing dog brings a new feeling of independence. Owners can be alerted to a baby's cry, a knock at the door, or a fire alarm. Since the majority of these dogs are rescued from local animal shelters, training programs also help to create useful and productive lives for these animals. Most important is the fact that hearing dogs also bring companionship and love to their owners.

Trained hearing dogs can be recognized in public by their orange collar, leash, and vest. To receive more information about hearing dogs and training centers, write to the following:

National Center for Hearing Dog
Information
The American Humane Association
East Hampden Avenue
Denver, CO 80231

Jennifer Orme
Coordinator
The National Center for
Hearing Dog Information

CHAPTER ONE

A Christmas Present

Can you imagine what it would be like to be put in a box and given away as a present on Christmas Day? This is exactly what happened to the dog in this story.

He was born on a farm. At first he lived with his brothers and sisters in a basket under the kitchen table. But when the puppies started to run around, the farmer's wife said, "Enough! Out! These puppies are going to trip me. They must go out to the barn where they won't be under my feet."

So for the next two or three weeks the puppies romped and chased each other around the barn, and slept on some straw and a blanket in the corner.

Their mother was a beautiful collie who helped with the sheep on the farm. The

puppies weren't quite sure who their father was, but they overheard the farmer say they were "a handsome assortment of mixed breeds" and they felt this was a very fine thing to be. In fact, their father was a terrier, so some of the puppies had long silky coats like their mother, and some were wiry and looked more like their father. They were a mixed bunch.

Then, one chilly day when they were about eight weeks old, one little puppy found himself being lifted up and placed in a cardboard box.

"Help! Help!" he wimpered, as he scratched at the sides of the box. He was even more frightened when the carton rattled and shook. Later he realized he must have traveled in a car, but at the time he knew nothing of cars.

The box was carried into a house, and when it was opened, the frightened little puppy saw to his surprise that he was under a tree covered with colored lights. Strange smells and noises were all around. He jumped out of the box, and, when hands tried to capture him, he ran into a corner.

There he sat, trembling with fright, under a chair.

He didn't notice at first, but a boy was sitting on the chair. A hand came down and very gently stroked the puppy's head. In return, the puppy licked the boy's hand.

"Look, he's gone straight to Philip," someone said.

In a few moments the puppy was on Philip's lap. The boy was quiet, sitting somehow apart from everyone else in the crowded room. The puppy licked him again and snuggled up to sleep in his arms. While all the others rushed around opening presents, chattering and eating, the quiet boy and the puppy stayed together.

The two other children in the family, Elizabeth and John, were both slightly jealous that the puppy made friends with Philip so quickly. They wanted to hold him as well, and to carry him around. Elizabeth was only four, and when she did have a chance to pick him up, she squeezed his ribs so hard he ran quickly back to Philip again.

The puppy's only real memory of his first Christmas Day was making friends with

Philip. He forgot how, when he was first put out in the garden, he hated the feel of the wet grass under his paws, and how he raced back into the house again. He forgot that when he was first placed in a basket with a bright, new, red blanket he jumped out again, as he didn't realize this was his bed. Nor did he remember being given little pieces of turkey mixed in with his canned dog food — although at the time he thought it delicious.

After the turkey he felt much braver and

ventured into the middle of the room, where he found a present that had not been opened. It was soft, and so he shook it, growling fiercely, as if it were a mouse. Everyone laughed at him, and he ran once more to Philip for safety and comfort.

That night, when he was left in the kitchen in his new basket with the red blanket, he whimpered and cried, for he was lonely. He did not understand he was the best Christmas present that the children had ever been given. All he knew was that he wanted to go back to the farm and curl up in the straw with his brothers and sisters and his mother.

After a while Philip's father came down into the kitchen. He gave the sad puppy a hug and placed an old windup alarm clock in the basket, covering it with a corner of the red blanket. He then put the puppy gently back in the basket and gave him a dog biscuit.

"Now you must sleep, little puppy," he said. "The clock may not be warm like your mother, but the ticking might stop you from feeling so lonely."

The puppy ate the biscuit slowly, crunching each bit carefully with his needle-sharp teeth, and settled down. The clock ticking was indeed a friendly sound. And so at last, dreaming of Christmas trees and presents, and especially of his new friend Philip, the little puppy slept.

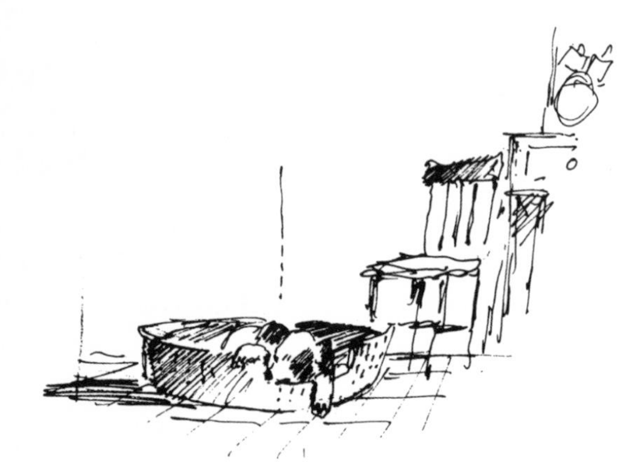

CHAPTER TWO

Give A Dog A Name

During the next few days the family all argued about what to call the new puppy. He was mostly white, with brown patches on his back and one big black patch over his left eye. This made him look both rather comic and a little fierce.

"Why don't we call him Sinbad, or Captain Flint?" the father suggested.

"I think we should call him Tiny," Elizabeth said.

"Don't be silly," said John. "He might grow into an enormous dog."

"We could try Patch," the mother suggested.

Everyone shook their heads.

"Or Wag?" said the father. "He's always wagging his tail."

The puppy wagged his tail at all these suggestions, for he could see they were talking about him. He really wanted Philip to be the one to choose his name. But Philip never joined in these discussions. In fact, Philip never talked at all.

In the end, Elizabeth came up with the right name.

"Let's call him Buttons," she said. "He's always trying to eat our buttons."

It was true. Whenever they lifted him up he chewed their buttons if he could.

The name seemed to suit him, and very quickly he learned to look up whenever he heard, "Buttons! Buttons!"

He learned lots of other things in those first few weeks, too. He jumped into his basket whenever someone said, "Basket!" in a firm voice. He was quickly house-broken and enjoyed going out into the garden whatever the weather. It was full of exciting smells, and he used to bark at the cats next door. He liked digging holes in the flowerbeds and the lawn, but this made the family angry.

"No! No!" they shouted, and Buttons

would creep into his basket until they had forgiven him.

Nor was he popular on the occasions when he took a shoe or slipper to his basket to chew. The leather tasted marvelous, just as good as any bone. It made his mouth feel good, too, where new teeth were coming through. But he was always scolded when he chewed shoes. Then he would run to Philip. Philip was always kind to him.

But why didn't Philip talk, like the others talked?

CHAPTER THREE

The Boy Who Didn't Talk

Buttons noticed other things about Philip. For instance, Philip did not seem to know when Buttons barked or scratched at a door if Philip couldn't see him. Also, Buttons discovered he could wake Philip each morning by bounding onto the bed, but not by barking or whining on the floor.

Buttons was an intelligent little dog, and before long he worked out for himself that Philip couldn't hear.

Buttons was right. Philip had been born deaf, profoundly deaf in fact, which meant he could hear almost nothing at all. This makes learning to speak very difficult.

In every other way Philip was a normal boy. He could run and climb trees, and throw sticks and balls. He got hungry and tired like other boys. But like many deaf people, he was lonely. He found it hard to join in games when John and Elizabeth had other children around, and until Buttons came he used to spend a lot of time by himself. Now he was happy, as he and the puppy understood each other. Neither of them could talk, but each had his own way of communicating, and they could be seen playing together for hours.

What Buttons didn't realize at first was that Philip's mother was also deaf. She had learned to talk, and with the use of a hearing aid she could hear quite a lot. She could understand what other people said, too, by lipreading: following the way their lips shaped words as they were talking. She knew the problems that Philip faced and helped him as much as she could.

Philip's teachers helped him, too. He went to a special school for deaf children. A bus came for him every day during the school year. Buttons used to stand at the window with his tail between his legs and watch the bus drive away. He was always waiting for Philip when he returned. He would leap into the boy's arms and lick his chin. Then they would spend the rest of the day happily together.

CHAPTER 4

A Porcupine

One warm spring day in March, Buttons found a porcupine at the bottom of the garden. He sniffed at it, and the porcupine curled into a ball. Ouch! He hurt his nose on the prickles. He then ran around and around it in circles, barking wildly.

John and Elizabeth came out to see what was going on. When they saw the porcupine still curled up in a tight little ball, they were afraid that Buttons would hurt it or that the porcupine would hurt Buttons. They tried to call Buttons away, but he took no notice of them.

John ran for help. His parents came, followed by Philip.

"Here, boy! Here, Buttons!" said the father sternly. Buttons kept on barking, as if he hadn't heard. Philip then tugged at his collar, but still Buttons wouldn't leave the porcupine alone.

Then Buttons heard a new noise. He knew at once that Philip had made it. He stopped and looked around. Philip made the noise again. It was no more than a grunt from the back of his throat. Buttons knew, though, that this was important, and he went to Philip and licked him.

Philip's parents noticed and they made a great fuss of both Philip and Buttons.

"Philip talked!" Elizabeth said. "Philip talked!"

No one noticed the porcupine slip away, but by the time they all stopped looking at Philip and Buttons it had gone.

A few days later Philip's teacher came to the house. Buttons could tell they were talking about him. Now Philip's father took Buttons to the other end of the room and held him firmly by the collar while the teacher tried to make Philip call him.

Philip waved his hand as he always did when he wanted Buttons to come. But Buttons couldn't go as the father held on firmly to his collar. Again and again Philip waved his hand, but Buttons was always held back. Both boy and dog were puzzled.

Then they went down to the garden where Buttons had found the porcupine. Once more they tried to make Philip call Buttons. Suddenly, Philip knew what they wanted. He made the same noise he had

made before. Immediately, Buttons's collar was released, and he ran to Philip and licked him. They repeated this several times.

That evening everyone in the family was happy, for Philip had started to talk.

"It's all because of Buttons," said Elizabeth.

CHAPTER FIVE

A Sad Picnic

Buttons was not more than nine months old when the family took him on a vacation. They rented a house near the sea, and every day they all went to a beach.

It wasn't much fun for Buttons. The sea was salty, which he didn't like, and the sand got everywhere and made his skin tickle. Once they forgot to take fresh water for him to drink, and he was expected to drink orange soda pop when he was thirsty. He didn't like that at all. Their sandwiches, too, if he got a chance to eat one, were always gritty and tasted of sand.

If Philip hadn't been there Buttons would have hated every minute of it. As it was, Philip enjoyed digging in the sand and exploring the rocks at low tide and swimming, so Buttons stayed close to him and made the best of it. More and more now Philip talked to Buttons, developing a language which both boy and dog seemed to understand.

It had taken them a whole day to drive to the house near the sea. On the way, they had stopped for a picnic in a large park. The children had played in the tall green ferns and grasses, and Buttons had raced around with them. When the vacation was over, to Buttons's delight, they stopped at the same picnic place on their return trip.

Once more the children ran along the little paths and through the green ferns, playing hide-and-seek. Buttons, as always, stayed close to Philip. Then, to Buttons's joy, a rabbit ran off in front of him. In a flash he was after it. What bliss! Buttons had never chased rabbits before, and now he forgot everything with the excitement of it all. Chasing rabbits was the most wonderful thing he had ever done!

Later, much later, Buttons vaguely remembered hearing the family calling him, but he took no notice. He was just about to catch a rabbit at the time, and now, white tail and all,

it disappeared down a hole in the ground. In a frenzy he tried to follow it, but the hole was too small.

"Just you wait, little rabbit! Just you wait!" thought Buttons, as he started to dig.

Earth flew, paws scrabbled, and the hole grew bigger and bigger. Buttons dug on. Now he found he could get right down the hole. It was a tight squeeze, but he wriggled on and on down the dark tunnel. The smell of rabbits was everywhere, and thrilling beyond belief. All thoughts of Philip and his family had gone. He only thought RABBIT.

At last Buttons began to get hungry. He tried to get out of the hole. Going backwards was not so easy, as it dragged his hair the wrong way. Suddenly, he found he couldn't move forwards or backwards. His collar was caught on a tree root deep under the ground. He was stuck down the hole. No one could hear him bark, and he was miles from home.

Back at the picnic place the family searched and searched for him, calling and whistling. Even Philip called him, in his own way. They still had a long way to go, so at last the father drove to the nearest town and reported Buttons's loss at the police station.

"He is wearing a collar with a metal tag giving our address," he told the police.

"It he turns up, we'll contact you. Don't you worry."

The policeman was kind and tried to make them all feel better. But it was a sad, sad family that drove home that evening. In the back of the car Philip wept, for he had lost the best friend he had ever known.

CHAPTER SIX

Lost Dog

Poor Buttons! How he struggled underneath the earth to get free, but the more he pulled, the more his collar seemed to get caught. His paws became sore from scrabbling, and his eyes hurt from all the mud that got in them.

Eventually he fell into a fitful sleep. Hunger woke him, and he tried again to get free. Throughout the night and the next morning Buttons struggled, rested, and struggled, rested, and struggled again in the dark.

Then, when he was weak from hunger, thirst, and exhaustion, there was a "snap." His collar had broken. Buttons backed up the rabbit hole and into the fresh air. For some time he lay there, panting, too tired to move. He knew, though, what he had to do.

When he felt a little stronger he went straight to the picnic place where he had last seen his family. It was deserted. There was no car, no family, no Philip.

"They'll come back for me," he thought, and he sat down to wait. He did not realize how long he has been down the rabbit hole and that by now Philip and his family were over a hundred miles away.

After a long wait, when no one had come, Buttons set off in search of food and home. At first he kept to the road. But cars were traveling along very fast, and one nearly hit him. Now he was really frightened. He jumped into a ditch, and after a while set off across some fields. He didn't know he was going further and further from the town where his loss had been reported at the police station.

He passed several gardens, but none of them was his. They didn't smell right. On and on went Buttons. He drank from some rather dirty puddles, and in one garden he found some food that had been put out for a

cat. He wolfed it down, but, apart from that, he found nothing to eat. He sniffed around some garbage cans, but the people in the house shouted at him to go away. He crept up to the next house, too desperate to care if they were friendly or not, and lay down in the driveway.

A woman called out, "George, come and look here. There's a dog by the back door." She stroked Buttons and he tried to lick her hand, "Poor thing. I'll get you some milk," she said kindly.

"I think we should ask Charlie if the Animal Shelter will take him in. Charlie's worked there for years, he'll know what to do," her husband suggested. "But there's no harm in giving the dog something to eat first. He's in a bad way, poor little thing. He's not much more than a puppy, either."

Buttoms found himself shut in a shed. It reminded him of the farm where he'd been born. He was given a bowl of food and then he slept on an old blanket in the corner.

He was awakened by kind hands stroking him, and he heard a new voice say, "I'll take him to the Animal Shelter and see if anyone claims him. He's a nice-looking dog, and it's my guess that he's only been living outside for a few days. Come on, boy," Charlie added kindly to Buttons, and he lifted him into a basket, which he then carried to his van.

CHAPTER SEVEN

New Friends

Buttons was taken to a huge building and placed in a cage. There were dogs in other cages all around him. The noise of barking and whining came from every direction, but Buttons was too tired for it to disturb his sleep.

After a few days at the Animal Shelter, with regular food and frequent runs in the exercise yard, he was feeling more like his old self. When a visitor walked down between the cages with the attendant, Buttons pricked up his ears and wagged his tail eagerly.

"A nice, bright pup here," the newcomer said.

The cage door was opened, and they took Buttons away from the other dogs and gave him various orders. Buttons, always anxious

to please and quick to learn, sat when they told him. He ran to them when they called, and he turned his head quickly when they whistled or called from several directions.

"He's got good hearing and is extremely alert," the visitor said. "Do you know where he came from?"

"He was brought in by Charlie, one of the people who works here. He was found by Charlie's neighbors, half-starved and with no collar."

"I'll take him then," the visitor said. "He is just the dog we are looking for," and he put Buttons in his blue van.

Buttons trusted this tall, gentle man who seemed to understand dogs. As he sat in the van with him, he thought, "I do hope he is taking me home. How can I tell him Philip needs me?"

His new friend, who was called Tony, drove for about an hour, and finally they turned into a yard where there were several buildings. Buttons was taken inside one that looked rather like a stable and put into a pen. There was a big bed for him and a bowl of water. There were two other dogs, also in their own shoulder-high pens.

"We're going to teach you all sorts of things," said Tony kindly, "but we won't start lessons until tomorrow."

Buttons wagged his tail. He felt sure they were going to be kind to him here, and he wanted to please Tony if he could.

That evening he got to know his two companions. Like him, they were both mixed breeds and had been found by Tony at rescue centers after being abandoned.

Duke, the largest, who had a lot of German Shepherd in him, had been deliberately left miles from home. He had been loved as a small puppy, but his owners had stopped caring about him when he grew too big. They thought he ate too much, and he knocked things over in the tiny apartment where they lived. One day, they left him miles from home, and he was found and handed in to the police, who took him to a home for lost dogs.

Beauty was half Labrador and half spaniel. She was black with curly hair and floppy ears and rather long legs. Her owner, an old lady, had died, and she had lived for a few months with a family who had now gone to live in Australia. They had taken her to an animal shelter and asked them to find a good home for her. Then Tony came along and selected her.

Duke and Beauty had only been there for a few days and they were not entirely sure why Tony wanted them. Like Buttons, they had to wait to find out.

CHAPTER EIGHT

Training

Buttons's life changed completely now. The first thing that happened was that he was given a new name. Tony came in the next morning and said to him, "Right. From now on your name is Jogger." He repeated the name, "Jogger," "Jogger" several times. Whenever Buttons pricked up his ears or came to him after he said this name, he was given a tasty little biscuit.

"You'll soon get used to it," Tony encouraged. "All the dogs here are given new names, as we never know what they were called before."

Buttons quickly learned to answer to "Jogger," but he didn't really like it.

"I'll always think of myself as Buttons," he thought. "I wonder why Tony chose the name 'Jogger' for me?"

Almost as though he could read his thoughts, Tony said one day, "Don't blame me if you don't like your name. I didn't choose it."

"More and more mysterious," thought Buttons.

Once Buttons had gotten used to his new name, he was shown a squeaky ball that Tony always carried. Each time Tony made it squeak, Buttons had to go to him. Again, he was rewarded with a tasty little biscuit whenever he did so. After a few days it became second nature to go straight to Tony as soon as he heard the squeak.

Buttons was also given obedience lessons. Some things, like sitting when he was told, he had been taught before. Now he had to sit both when he heard the command and when Tony gave a special hand signal. In the same way, he was expected to lie down to a spoken order and at a hand signal. He had to "come" whenever Tony clapped his hands, as well as when he pressed the squeaky ball.

When he was on a leash he was taught always to walk on Tony's left side and not to pull. If he went down to the town he was expected to stop at the curb and wait quietly until it was safe to cross the road.

Duke and Beauty were being trained in the same way. All three were taught to pick up anything that Tony dropped, like a glove or a paper, and bring it to him. They were all encouraged not to bark. This was especially hard for Buttons, who had always enjoyed the sound of his own voice.

CHAPTER NINE

Alarms and Bells

After some weeks Buttons was taken into a cottage that was in the yard where he lived. To his surprise no one lived there, although part of it was furnished like a home, with a living room, dining room, kitchen, and bedroom. His training now took place in these rooms, and he was taught new skills.

When an alarm clock rang Buttons was expected to put his front legs on the bed in the bedroom, or jump onto the bed and wake up whoever was sleeping there. When he was used to doing this, he was taught to come in from another room whenever he heard the alarm, first pushing open the bedroom door before waking up the person in the bed.

If the door bell rang, he was taught to get

Tony and take him to the door. It was the same with the telephone. When it rang, he had to take Tony to it. Also, if the kitchen timer on the oven went off Buttons had to take Tony to the oven.

None of this was so very different from what he had done with Philip and his mother. He has always awakened Philip by bounding onto his bed, and he remembered going to Philip's mother and trying to tell her if someone was at the door. Most of the time she didn't know he was barking, so he had learned to tell her by wagging his tail and pawing at her leg.

"You're quick, all right, Jogger," said Tony one day. "It's almost as if you had worked with deaf people before."

Now Buttons understood, partly, at least, what was going on. He pricked up his ears and wagged his tail as he looked at Tony with pleasure.

Throughout the autumn their training continued. It was the same for all three. Then Duke was taught to respond to a baby's crying. Whenever he heard the noise he had to get Tony and take him to the baby's crib in the bedroom. Neither Buttons nor Beauty were taught this. "Perhaps Duke is going to a home with a baby and we are not," thought Buttons, using his intelligence once again.

There was one further lesson all three dogs were taught. Sometimes a fire alarm went off if there was a lot of smoke in the house. It gave a high-pitched continual ringing sound, and the dogs learned that this was different from all the other bells they had been trained to respond to. Whenever they heard the fire alarm they were expected to wake up the person in the bed, but not to take him anywhere. They had to continue to lie on the floor to show that this was something different. This meant danger.

There were often visitors at the training center, and Tony demonstrated to them what Buttons could do. Buttons enjoyed showing off a little and doing it all extra well. A lady said, "My, I don't believe we have ever had such a quick little dog to train where I come from." Buttons, you may be sure, wagged his tail with pride.

One day a group of children came to see Buttons. He understood from what they said

that their school had all saved up money to pay for his training. They had been asked to name him, and because most of the money they raised had come from a sponsored jogging race they had chosen the name Jogger.

"That explains it," thought Buttons, "but I still wish they'd chosen a nicer name."

CHAPTER TEN

Happy Christmas

Christmas was getting close, and all three dogs were ready to go to their new homes. Beauty and Duke left first. Each was given a special orange collar and leash, which is the symbol used by dogs that have completed their training with a hearing dog program. Also, they were given certificates to show they could go on public transportation, like dogs for the blind.

Gillian, who worked with Tony at the center for Hearing Dogs for the Deaf, took them to their new homes. While Tony was responsible for training the dogs, her job was to make all the arrangements with the families where the dogs were going, and to work with the deaf owners for about a week, explaining what each dog could do, and making sure the dog responded to the new owner. Buttons overheard her telling Tony how well both Duke and Beauty had settled down, and how useful they were.

He also heard her say that his new family wanted him to arrive as close to Christmas Day as possible. He hoped this meant he was going to a home with children.

At last, on Christmas Eve, he was given his new orange collar and leash and was driven away by Gillian. For two hours Buttons sat in the car and thought how sad it was that he always lost his best friends — first Philip, and now Tony.

Then the car drew up outside a house, a house Buttons knew well. There, waiting on the doorstep, were Philip, John, and Elizabeth.

Gillian was rather surprised to see a well-trained dog jump straight into a strange boy's arms. Philip and Buttons were so delighted to see each other again, they didn't notice the fuss going on all around them.

"It's Buttons. It's Buttons. I know it's Buttons," Elizabeth kept saying.

Meanwhile, Gillian was talking to Philip's

mother. "It's quite extraordinary. We trained the dog for you, not for your son, although of course we knew he was deaf, too."

"Quite," said Philip's father. "It was only when we had Buttons that we realized how much a dog can help a deaf person. Buttons was marvelous with Philip, but at the same time he was a real companion to my wife during the day, and helped her in all sorts of ways, although he wasn't trained. After we lost Buttons we thought we would never find another dog that was so intelligent, so we applied to the hearing dog organization for a trained dog."

At last peace was restored. Buttons stopped licking everyone, and they all stopped hugging Buttons. Gillian showed them how Buttons had been trained and said she would come back right after Christmas and work with them for about a week, until Buttons was fully settled again and using his training.

The next day was like Buttons's first Christmas, only better. The Christmas tree was there again, with its colored lights and the presents underneath. The turkey for Christmas dinner was as delicious as before. Buttons's basket was in the kitchen, with a new blanket in it, for the family had thought they were getting a new dog. When he went to sleep that night, Buttons was deeply contented for the first time in months, as he was home once more where he really belonged.

Upstairs, Philip thought, "There has never been a happier boy."

CHAPTER ELEVEN

A Famous Dog

Buttons's story does not end there.

He did everything he was trained to do extremely well, and was a tremendous help to Philip's mother, and to Philip when he wasn't at school. Philip was talking much more now and had several friends at school.

Some days Buttons went to school with Philip to show other families what a dog trained by a hearing dog program can do. Tony used to come to these demonstrations, and Buttons was always delighted to see him.

Then one day, a movie company called up and talked to Philip's father for a long time. The director had heard about Buttons and wanted to make a movie about him. Philip's father agreed.

For several weeks, people came and went from Philip's home. There were lighting technicians and sound technicians, a camera crew, a director and a producer and their assistants, and many other people besides. The family got used to a crowded house, and behaved as naturally as possible while they were being filmed.

The film was shown on television, and Buttons became a celebrity overnight.

Now he was invited to dog shows to demonstrate his skills. He was recognized everywhere. He was also asked to visit several schools where the students were interested in raising money to train more dogs. Philip and his mother went to all these places with Buttons, and they became celebrities, too.

Buttons's face, with the famous black patch over one eye, was used to advertise boxes of dog biscuits, and the money the company paid was turned over to the hearing dog program, to train even more dogs. A book was written about Buttons, and the story of how he had gotten lost was told in full, as well as how he was picked out by Tony at the Animal Shelter and trained.

Like all celebrities, he had a full and busy life, but he was never happier than when he was at home with the family he loved so much.

You may not believe in miracles, but you can believe in luck. It was a lucky day for Philip when Buttons first came to his home, and it was a lucky day for Buttons when he came back home to Philip. If ever Buttons has to be given a third name, perhaps it should be Lucky.

Other books by Linda Yeatman that you will enjoy reading:

Perkins, The Cat Who Was More Than A Friend
Pickles

About The Author

Linda Yeatman lives in Cambridge with her husband, three daughters, one dog, and two cats. She is a freelance journalist, and has written a number of books for children. She regularly reviews both children's and adult fiction.

About The Illustrator

Sir Hugh Casson lives in London with his wife, and has three daughters. He is internationally renowned as an architect, and until recently was the President of the Royal Academy. Sir Hugh is a prolific watercolor painter, and has written and illustrated a number of books both for children and for adults.

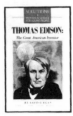